The Same Only Different

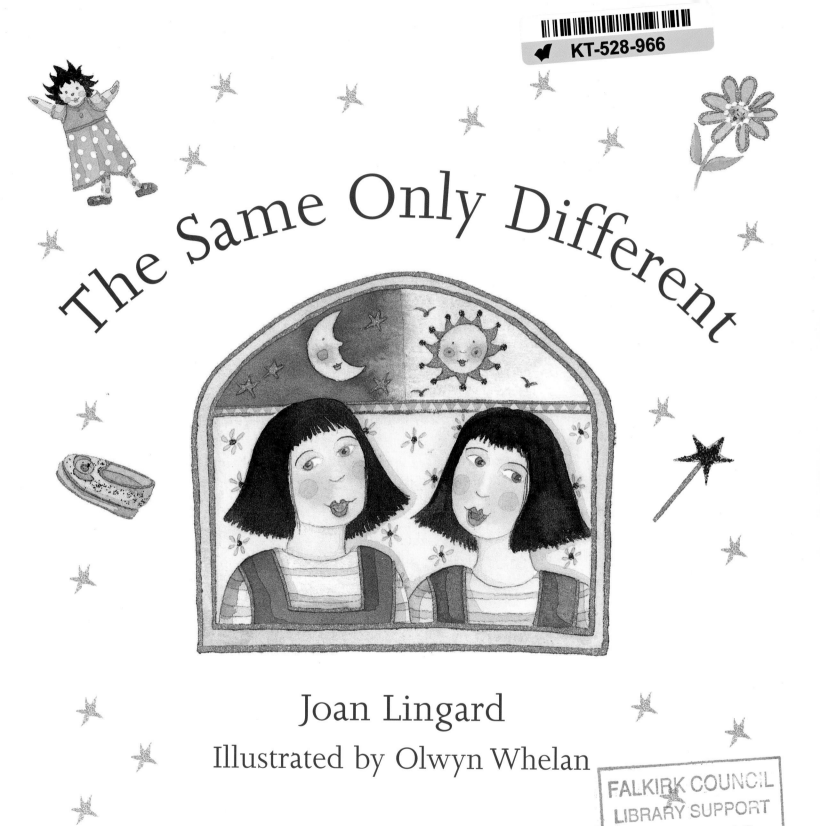

Joan Lingard

Illustrated by Olwyn Whelan

Glowworm Books

Sally-Sue and Polly-Prue are twins.
As alike as two pins,
From the tips of their toes to the tops of their heads.
So everyone said.

This book belongs to

Text © Joan Lingard
Illustrations © Olwyn Whelan

Published in 2001 by
Glowworm Books Ltd. Unit 7, Greendykes Industrial Estate,
Broxburn, West Lothian, EH52 6PG, Scotland

Telephone: 01506-857570
Fax: 01506-858100
E-Mail: admin@glowwormbooks.co.uk
URL: http://www.glowwormbooks.co.uk

ISBN 1-871512-64-6

Printed and bound by Scotprint Ltd, Haddington

Page layout by Mark Blackadder

Reprint Code   10   9   8   7   6   5   4   3   2   1

But that is not true
For Polly-Prue
Is different to Sally-Sue.

Can you tell the difference?
Now here is a clue: –
Sally-Sue has a smaller mouth and a longer nose than Polly-Prue.

They like to play games
And mix up their names,
'I'm Sally,' cries Polly-Prue.
'I'm Polly,' cries Sally-Sue.

But you know that's not true,
For they can't fool you.
You know which is Sally-Sue
And which is Polly-Prue.

Whose eyes are green and whose are blue?

Their mother says it's nice to be twins
As alike as two pins.
She likes to dress them the same
For, after all, she knows each by name.

But once she goes out
The twins give a shout.
They run to the wardrobe to see what's there,
And pull out dresses that they'd rather wear.

The dresses look the same but they're not.
Can you tell the difference?

The twins cry 'Hooray'.
For today is the day
They go to the park,
To swing on the swings and have a real lark.

Lots of things in the park look the same,
But they're different.
Can you tell which they are?

On Saturday they go downtown to shop
For socks and shoes and – if they're lucky – a lollipop.
They ride in on the bus and sit up top.
And then Father says, 'This is our stop!'

Three buses in a row and each one different.
Can you tell the difference?

'Look at the shoes!' cries Sally-Sue.
Her sister says, 'I want mine to be blue.'
So many shoes
It's hard to choose.

So many shoes and they're all different.
Can you tell the difference?

On Saturday they have money to spend,
They wish that Saturday would never end!

The sweet shop makes them goggle and stare.
So many sweets, so many treats are there.

So many sweets. Can you tell the difference?

The baker's shop is next on the list,
That is something not to be missed.

Mother says, 'We'll take a brown and a white.
Those two loaves should be about right.'

How many different loaves of bread can you see?

'Now,' says Mother, 'your hair needs to be cut.'
Father says, 'Remember, keep your eyes shut.'

The twins wail
To no avail.
Snip!. go the scissors, snippety-snip
Snippety, snippety, snip.

Their hair looks the same but it's not.
Can you tell the difference?

They go to a cafe as a special treat
For something to drink and something to eat.

The twins have juice and little round cakes
A bit like the ones their mother makes.

Their cakes look the same but they're different and so is the juice.
Can you tell the difference?

'It's been a long day,'
That's what Mum and Dad say.
'It's time to sleep,
So not another cheep!'

And next Saturday is their BIRTHDAY!
What can you see in the bedroom that is the same only different?

Happy birthday Polly Prue
Happy birthday Sally-Sue
Happy birthday dear twin-pins
Happy birthday to you!

So many cards and so many presents
And they're all different.
Can you tell the difference?
The cakes look the same too, but they're not, are they?

Now that they're five it's time to start school.
They arrive at nine, as is the rule.

The teacher says, 'How nice to have twins
As alike as two pins!
Though we may have some bother
Telling one from the other.'

The girls and boys think Sally-Sue
Looks just the same as Polly-Prue.

They can't tell the difference. But you can, can't you?
If you need a clue look back to page two!